To my father-in-law
grumpy grandad Len
- S S

For G.R. hero
with love
- C B

Copyright © 2009 by Good Books, Intercourse, PA 17534
International Standard Book Number: 978-1-56148-669-4

Library of Congress Catalog Card Number: 2009004884

Text copyright © Steve Smallman 2009
Illustrations copyright © Cee Biscoe 2009

Original edition published in English by Little Tiger Press,
an imprint of Magi Publications, London, England, 2009

Printed in China

Library of Congress Cataloging-in-Publication Data

Smallman, Steve.
Gruff the Grump / Steve Smallman ; illustrated by Cee Biscoe.
p. cm.

Summary: When a grizzly bear, called Gruff the Grump by other animals, grudgingly
listens to a small rabbit's pleas for help, she thanks him with simple gifts that reveal
to him how dark and lonely his life has become.
ISBN 978-1-56148-669-4 (hardcover : alk. paper)

[1. Mood (Psychology)--Fiction. 2. Gifts--Fiction. 3. Bears--Fiction.
4. Rabbits--Fiction.] I. Biscoe, Celia, ill. II. Title.

PZ7.S639145Gru 2009
[E]--dc22
2009004884

GRUFF the GRUMP

Steve Smallman

Illustrated by Cee Biscoe

Good Books

Intercourse, PA 17534
800/762-7171
www.GoodBooks.com

Gruff was a bear.

A great big bear.

A great big, scowly, growly, grizzly grump of a bear.
He lived all alone in a musty, dusty old cave where nobody
ever came to visit.

The other animals hid when they saw him coming.
They called him "Gruff the Grump."
"HUMPH!" went Gruff the Grump,
to show he didn't care.

One morning, Gruff the Grump was stomping through the forest when he saw something strange . . .

It was a small, upside-down rabbit,
high in the branches of a tree.

"Hello, Mr. Bear," said the rabbit, upside-downly. "I'm a bit stuck. Can you help me down, please-thank you very much?"

"HUMPH!" scowled Gruff the Grump,
and he turned to walk away.

"Oh please, Mr. Bear, PLEEEEEEASE get me down!"
pleaded the rabbit.

Much to Gruff the Grump's surprise, he
found himself lifting the little rabbit
gently down to the ground.

"Thank you, thank you, Mr. Bear," said the rabbit.
"There was a fallen star caught in the tree so I had
to rescue it, but then I got stuck and then you
had to rescue me.

"Here," she said
with a smile,
"you can have it."

She carefully put the fallen star in the old bear's
huge, hairy paw and hopped off home.

Gruff the Grump thought that the "star" looked
a lot like a leaf, but he took it home anyway
and put it on his mantelpiece.

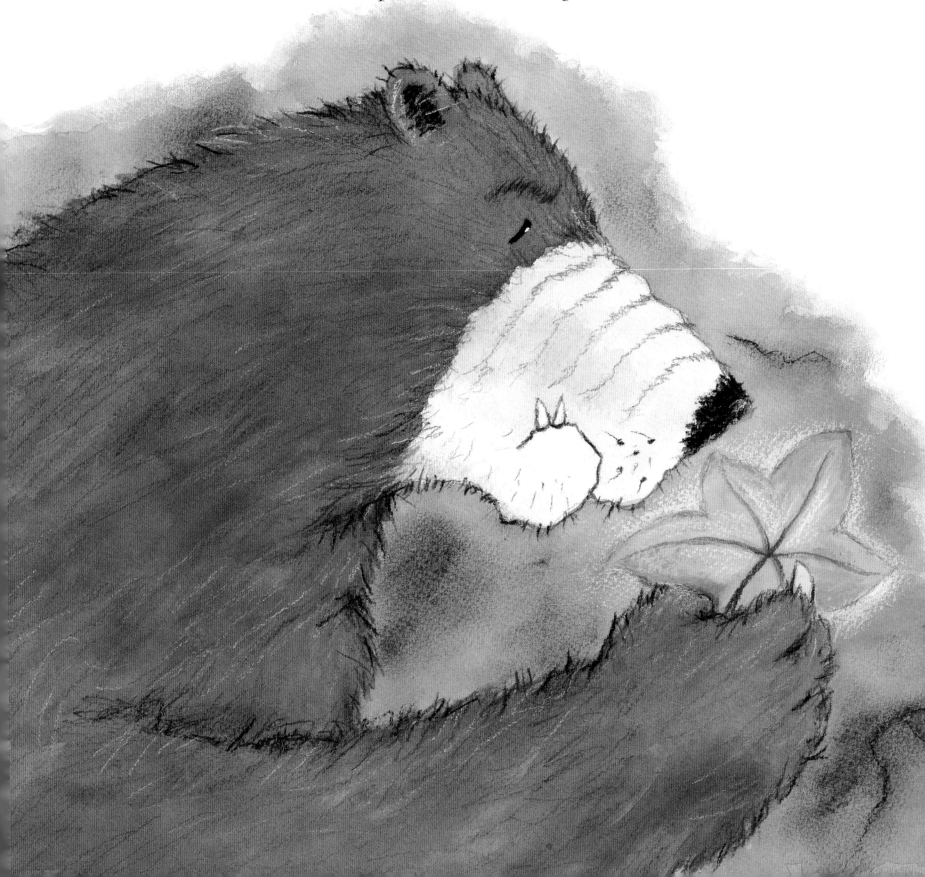

It was so golden and beautiful that it made him realize
just how musty and dusty his cave had become.

And for the first time in a very long time, he
dusted the mantelpiece and brushed away
some of the cobwebs.

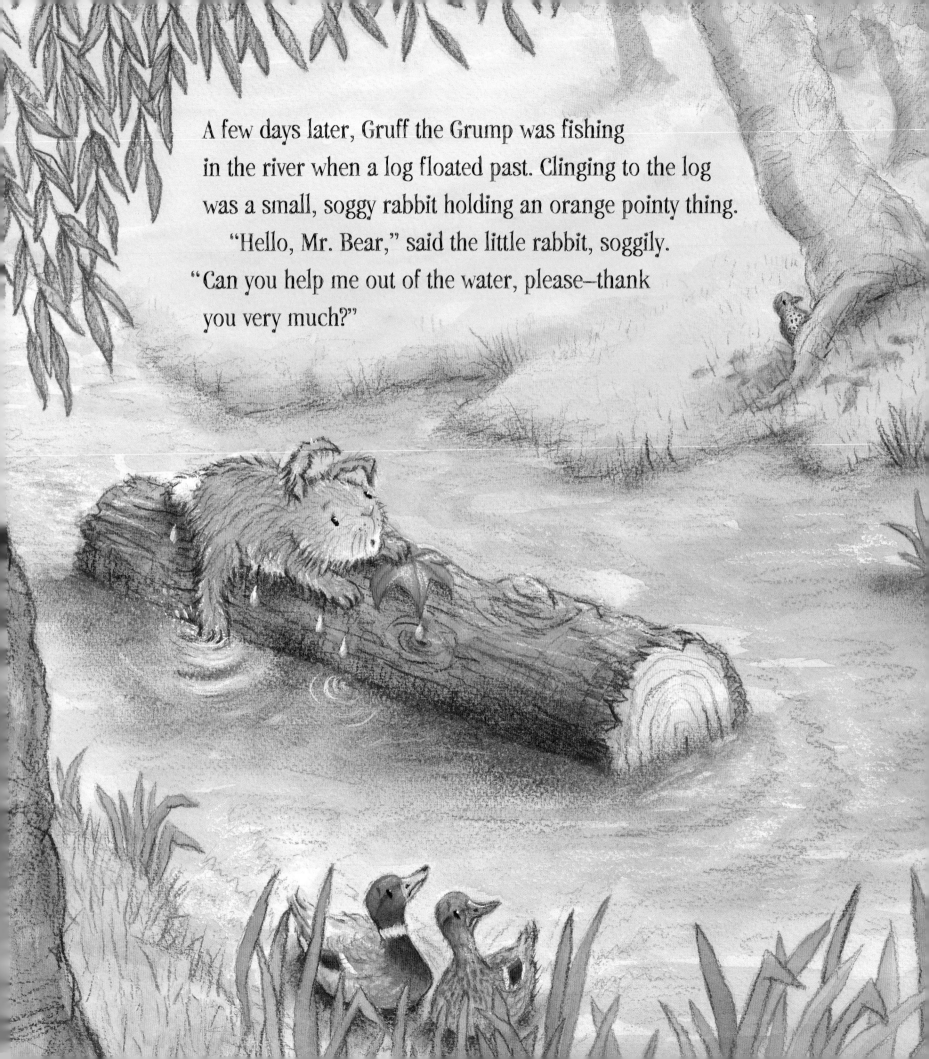

A few days later, Gruff the Grump was fishing
in the river when a log floated past. Clinging to the log
was a small, soggy rabbit holding an orange pointy thing.
"Hello, Mr. Bear," said the little rabbit, soggily.
"Can you help me out of the water, please—thank
you very much?"

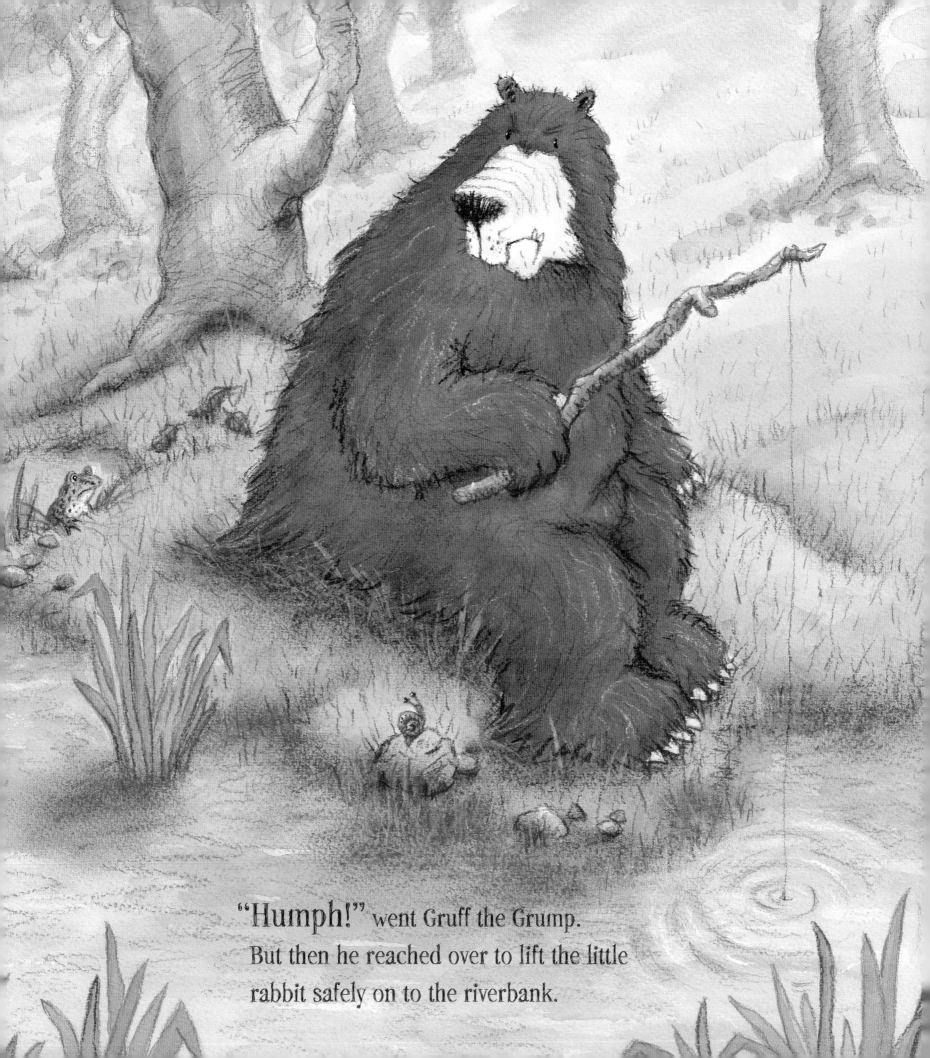

"Humph!" went Gruff the Grump.
But then he reached over to lift the little
rabbit safely on to the riverbank.

"Thank you, thank you, Mr. Bear,"
said the rabbit. "There was a fallen star
in the water and I had to rescue it.
You are very big and very kind.
Will you look after it for me?"

But Gruff the Grump just turned
and lumbered away. He was feeling
a bit funny. Nobody had ever, ever
called him "kind" before.
"But Mr. Bear, Mr. Bear,
come back!" cried the little rabbit,
running after him. "I can't look
after it on my own!"

"OKAY, OKAY, I'LL TAKE IT!"
snarled Gruff the Grump. And
snatching the star, he slammed
his cave door behind him.

Gruff the Grump put the star on the mantelpiece
next to his other star. They looked so clean and
colorful that they made him realize just how grim
and grimy his cave still was.

So for the first time in a very long time, he swept
up all the old pine needles from the floor.

Now his cave was very clean. But it was bare and empty inside, and suddenly Gruff felt like a bear who was empty inside too. He started to feel sad . . .

And when he'd finished feeling sad, he started to feel cross . . .

And he was right in the middle of feeling cross when there was a knock on the door.
"WHAT IS IT NOW?"
he shouted.

It was the little rabbit with a wheelbarrow full of stars.
"Hello, Mr. Bear," she said worn-outly.
"There were lots and lots of fallen stars and I had
to rescue them . . ."

"GO AWAY!" Gruff the Grump roared.
"I DON'T WANT ANY MORE
STUPID STARS!"

Then to his great surprise,
the little rabbit burst into tears.

Gruff the Grump felt terrible.
He wanted the little rabbit
to stop crying but he didn't
know what to do. He tried
pulling silly faces . . .
But that didn't work.

He did a funny dance . . .
But that didn't work either.

Then he sat down next to her and said,
"I'm sorry I shouted at you, little rabbit.
I really am a grizzly old grump of a bear."

The little rabbit stopped crying and tried
a little smile. And for the first time in a very
long time, Gruff the Bear smiled too!

Gruff and the little rabbit scattered the stars
around the cave, laughing out loud as they fell
like golden snowflakes all around them.

The little rabbit stayed and played with Gruff
until nearly bedtime.

"I have to go now," she said sadly.

"Will you come again soon?" asked Gruff.
"Very soon!" the little rabbit smiled.
Then she kissed him goodnight
and hopped off home.

Gruff the Bear gave a great big yawn and snuggled
down to sleep in his warm, starry bed.
And for the first time in a very long time,
he was happy.